Sophie
the Sapphire
Fairy

To Iola and Amany, who love
stories about fairies

Special thanks to
Linda Chapman

No part of this work may be reproduced, stored in a retrieval
system, or transmitted in any form or by any means, electronic,
mechanical, photocopying, recording, or otherwise, without written
permission of the publisher. For information regarding permission,
write to Rainbow Magic Limited, c/o HIT Entertainment,
830 South Greenville Avenue, Allen, TX 75002-3320.

ISBN-13: 978-0-439-93533-3
ISBN-10: 0-439-93533-4

12 11 10 9 8 7 6 5 4   9 10 11 12 13 14/0
Printed in the U.S.A.   40

First Scholastic printing, November 2007

Sophie
the Sapphire
Fairy

by Daisy Meadows

SCHOLASTIC INC.

New York   Toronto   London   Auckland
Sydney   Mexico City   New Delhi   Hong Kong

The Fairyland Palace

Adventure Playground

Tippington Manor

Tippington Town

The Tall Toy Store

Fountain

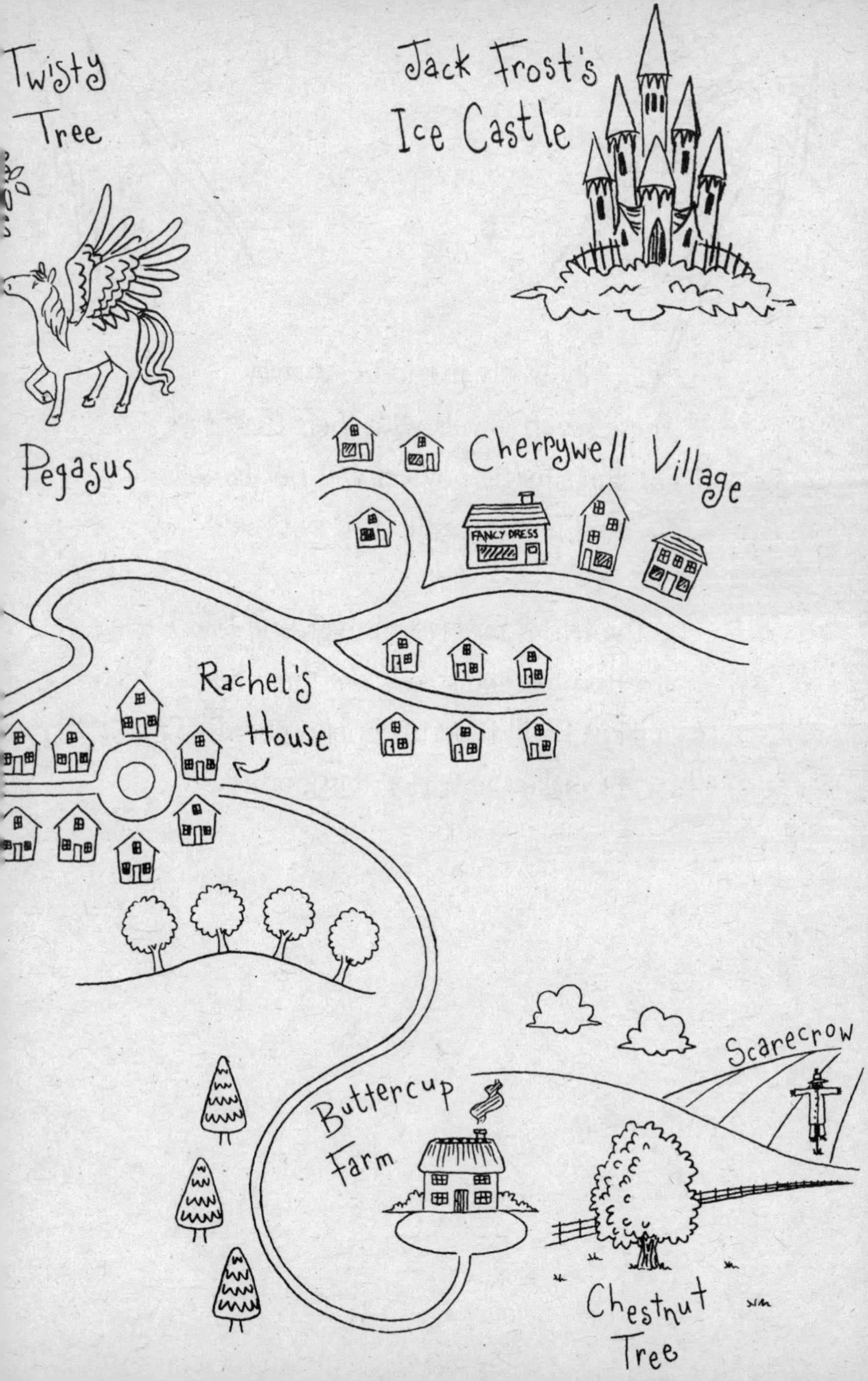

Twisty
Tree

Jack Frost's
Ice Castle

Pegasus

Cherrywell Village

FANCY DRESS

Rachel's
House

Buttercup
Farm

Scarecrow

Chestnut
Tree

By frosty magic I cast away
These seven jewels with their fiery rays,
So their magic powers will not be felt
And my icy castle shall not melt.

The fairies may search high and low
To find the gems and take them home.
But I will send my goblin guards
To make the fairies' mission hard.

Contents

Wishes in the Air

"I wish this rain would stop," Kirsty Tate said to her friend Rachel Walker as they splashed through the puddles on Main Street. "My sneakers are soaked!" She pulled her rainbow-colored umbrella further down over their heads.

"Mine, too," Rachel said. "But I'm glad we came into town today. I got the

perfect present for Danny's birthday
party next week." She swung the
shopping bag in her hand. It contained a
bright red, turbo-
charged squirt gun
that Rachel
was sure
Danny, her
six-year-old
cousin,
would love.
"I wish I was

going to be here for his party." Kirsty
sighed.

"Me, too. I can't believe you're going
home tomorrow," Rachel told her. "This
week went by so fast!"

"Too fast," replied Kirsty. "I just hope
we find another magic jewel today."

The two girls grinned at each other. They had an incredible secret. Rachel and Kirsty were best friends with the fairies! They'd helped the fairies out lots of times in the past, when Jack Frost had been causing trouble. Now they'd been asked to help again.

This time, mean Jack Frost had stolen seven magic jewels from Queen Titania's crown. The jewels controlled special fairy powers. Without them, the Jewel Fairies couldn't recharge their magic wands! But Jack Frost had hidden the jewels in the human world and had sent his goblin servants to guard them.

Rachel and Kirsty had already helped five of the Jewel Fairies get their magic jewels back. There were still two gems missing — the sapphire that controlled wishing magic, and the diamond that controlled flying magic. Rachel and Kirsty had to find them as soon as possible. The fairies' special jewel celebration was supposed to take place the very next day!

"We need to find the missing jewels by tomorrow," Kirsty said anxiously. "Maybe we should start looking for another one now."

"But you know what Queen Titania always says," Rachel reminded her.

Kirsty smiled. "Don't look for magic — let it find you."

Rachel nodded. "I guess we just have to wait and see what happens. Let's go home this way," she said, pointing down the street. "We can walk past the mermaid fountain."

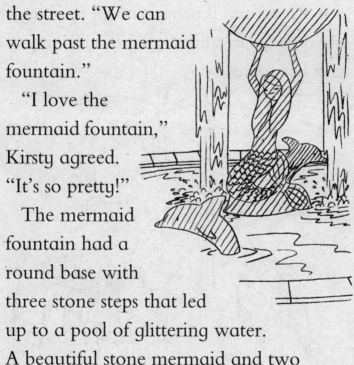

"I love the mermaid fountain," Kirsty agreed. "It's so pretty!"

The mermaid fountain had a round base with three stone steps that led up to a pool of glittering water. A beautiful stone mermaid and two

leaping dolphins had been carved into the
fountain. The mermaid's hands were raised
above her head, and she was holding a
large bowl. Water flowed over the sides
of the bowl and into the pool below.

As Kirsty and Rachel walked up, they
saw a little girl standing by the fountain
with her mom.

The girl sighed. "I wish I could have a dolphin of my own, Mom," she said, looking at the stone dolphins leaping around the beautiful mermaid.

The girls heard a faint tinkling sound in the air. Just then, a blue balloon came floating down from the sky toward the little girl. Rachel and Kirsty stared in amazement. The balloon was in the shape of a dolphin!

"Mom, look!" the girl squealed excitedly. "A dolphin balloon!"

Her mom grabbed the string of the balloon. "Wow, what a strange coincidence," she said, looking around to see if anyone might have lost it. But there was no one around, other than Rachel and Kirsty. She laughed. "It's almost like your wish came true, sweetheart!"

Rachel and Kirsty looked at each other with wide eyes. They were both thinking the same thing: Could the little girl's wish *really* have come true?

The girl and her mom hurried down the street with the balloon.

"Did you see the way that balloon appeared out of nowhere?" Kirsty whispered to Rachel.

"Yes, right after the little girl wished for a dolphin! Do you think . . . ?" Rachel broke off as a man walked toward the fountain with a little boy. They were both huddled under an umbrella.

"Can I throw a coin in the fountain and make a wish, Dad?" the boy asked.

His dad fished a penny out of the pocket of his jeans. "Catch, Tom!" he said with a grin, tossing the coin to his son. Tom caught the shiny penny and ran up the steps to the edge of the fountain.

"I wish the rain would stop so Dad and I could play football!" he cried.

As he threw the penny into the pool,

water splashed up. The water droplets caught in the air for a moment, and looked like they were glowing with a magical blue light. Again, the faint sound of bells seemed to echo through the air.

As Tom ran back down the steps, a ray of sunlight broke through the clouds. It lit up the gray stone fountain and made a rainbow in the rain. Then the gray clouds parted overhead. The rain slowly let up, then stopped completely.

"It stopped raining!"
Rachel exclaimed, staring
up at the sky.

Tom's dad also
looked up in surprise.
"What a quick
change in the
weather!" he
remarked.

"It was my wish!"
Tom cried. "The fountain must
be magic, Dad!"

His dad smiled at him. "Oh, Tom, you
know magic isn't real. Come on, let's go
home and get the football."

Rachel and Kirsty stared at each other.
No matter what Tom's dad said, they
knew the truth: Magic was real, and

wishes could come true. At least, they
could if there was a magical sapphire
nearby!

"Oh, Rachel!" Kirsty gasped as soon as
Tom and his dad were out of earshot.
"This means Sophie's magic sapphire
must be awfully close!"

The Mermaid's Secret

"You're right, Kirsty! The sapphire must be here somewhere," Rachel said. She glanced around. They were the only people near the fountain now. "Let's take a look."

Kirsty closed the umbrella. She put it down on one of the benches around the fountain. Then she took a quick look

underneath the bench, while Rachel
peeked behind the old-fashioned mailbox
next to it.

Psst!

Kirsty and Rachel jumped.

"What was that?" Kirsty asked.

"*Psst!* Over here!" a tiny voice called.

Rachel and Kirsty looked around wildly.

Where was the voice coming from?

"In the mailbox!" the voice giggled.

Both girls looked at the mailbox.
Sitting in the letter slot, swinging
her legs, was a
very tiny, very
pretty fairy.
She had long
black hair
held back in
a ponytail,
and she was
wearing a blue
skirt and top. She
waved at the girls.

"Hello, I'm Sophie the Sapphire Fairy,"
she said, smiling. "I've heard how much
you've helped the other Jewel Fairies. Will
you please help me find my sapphire?"

"Of course we will!" Kirsty replied.

"We just saw two children making wishes that came true," Rachel told the fairy.

"I know," Sophie replied. "It sounds like my sapphire is working its magic. Let's try to find it!"

Rachel began to hunt behind the bench, while Sophie flew around the mailbox.

"I'll go and look in the fountain," Kirsty called, running up the stone steps.

The bottom of the fountain's pool was covered with turquoise tiles, which made the water look really blue. Kirsty gazed up at the mermaid statue. It was even prettier up close! But then Kirsty noticed that the three cherubs climbing up the outside of the mermaid's bowl were the ugliest cherubs she'd ever seen. They had really long noses and beady eyes.

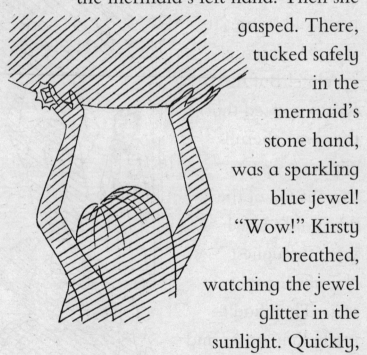

Suddenly, a flash of blue caught Kirsty's eye. It seemed to be coming from just underneath the bowl, right where the mermaid's hands were. Kirsty squinted at the mermaid's left hand. Then she gasped. There, tucked safely in the mermaid's stone hand, was a sparkling blue jewel! "Wow!" Kirsty breathed, watching the jewel glitter in the sunlight. Quickly, she slipped off her sneakers and rolled up her jeans.

The pool at the base of the fountain
was wide, but it wasn't very deep. Kirsty
could easily walk
through it to
reach the
statue. She
stepped into the
water. It was
very cold and
the tiles felt
slippery, but
she had to get
to the sapphire!
Keeping her
eyes firmly
fixed on the
jewel, Kirsty
began to wade through the water.

As she reached the mermaid, her heart

pounded with excitement. She stretched
up and gently pulled the twinkling
sapphire out of the mermaid's fingers.

Then she turned to call her friends. "Sophie! Rach — *arghhh!*" Kirsty was cut off as a blast of water came shooting at her from one of the cherubs above. It hit her right in the face!

Spluttering in surprise, Kirsty stared at the cherub. Her eyes widened as she noticed its pointy nose and huge feet. It wasn't part of the statue at all. It was one of Jack Frost's goblins!

Kirsty in Trouble

The goblin jumped up onto the top of the bowl. "That's Jack Frost's jewel!" he shouted. "Put it back right now, you pesky girl!"

Kirsty's heart hammered in her chest. To her horror, she saw that there was a second goblin on the fountain also disguised as a cherub. No wonder the

cherubs had looked so ugly! This
one was climbing down toward
her with a snarl on his face.

Kirsty turned to run,
but she was too
late. The goblin
reached out from
the fountain and
shoved her.
Kirsty cried
out as her feet
slipped on the
slimy tiles. She
fell into the water
with a splash. As
she landed, the sapphire
slipped from her hand and flew
through the air. It dropped into the pool
and sank out of sight.

Kirsty looked around frantically for the sapphire, but the tiles were so bright that she couldn't see the jewel against them. She felt around in the water. *Where is it?* she wondered. She had to find the sapphire before the goblins did! The two goblins jumped down from the fountain and splashed toward her, their beady eyes gleaming.

"Stay away!" Kirsty gasped, struggling to her feet. But the goblins began splashing water at her, so she couldn't see a thing.

Coughing and spluttering, Kirsty scrambled to the edge of the pool. She was soaked! Her hair was dripping and water was running down her face. Rachel ran up the steps with Sophie flying right behind her.

"Are you OK?" Rachel cried, helping Kirsty out of the water. "You're soaking

wet and —" She broke off with a gasp as
soon as she spotted the goblins. "Goblins!"
Kirsty nodded.

"Are you hurt?" Sophie asked anxiously.

"I'm fine, but the sapphire is in the pool
with the goblins," Kirsty replied, shivering.

"I found it in the mermaid's hand, but then I dropped it."

"You won't get the sapphire back!" one of the goblins yelled. "It's ours now." He nudged the other goblin. "Come on, snail-brain," he ordered. "Hurry up and find it!"

"I don't see why I have to do all the work," the other one grumbled. He gave the first goblin a shove. "You find it!"

"No, you!" the first goblin yelled, pushing him back.

"No! You do it!"

The water bubbled and foamed as the two goblins pushed each other around the pool, arguing loudly about who should look for the jewel.

"We'll never be able to get by those goblins and grab the sapphire. What are we going to do?" Sophie sighed. She landed on Rachel's shoulder as the two girls retreated down the steps to talk.

"I d-d-don't know," Kirsty said, her teeth chattering.

"You must be freezing," Rachel told Kirsty. "Put on my jacket."

"Thanks," Kirsty said gratefully. "I wish I was warm and dry."

Sophie gave a tinkling laugh. "I can fix that!" she declared. "I have just enough magic left in my wand for one small wish." She raised her wand and waved it over Kirsty's head. Blue and silver sparkles danced in the air. As they swirled down around Kirsty, a wave of warmth washed over her, starting at her head and sweeping all the way down to her toes.

"I'm dry again!" Kirsty gasped, looking down at her clothes. "Thanks, Sophie."

"No problem," replied the little fairy. She flew over and perched on Kirsty's dry shoulder. "Now, how are we going to get the sapphire back?"

Kirsty glanced over at Rachel. Her friend was staring at the shopping bag on

the bench with a thoughtful look on her
face. "Rachel?" Kirsty asked.

Rachel turned to face her friend,
her eyes shining. "I have a plan!"
she announced.

Into Battle!

"We'll use the umbrella and the shopping
bag to keep the goblins away while we
search for the jewel," Rachel said
eagerly. She noticed that Kirsty and
Sophie looked confused. "Sophie, you fly
into the air and drop the shopping bag
over the head of one goblin. That will
keep him busy for a while. Kirsty and I

can fight off the other goblin with the umbrella."

"Good plan," Sophie said, grinning. "Sounds like I'll be getting wet again," said Kirsty, sighing. Then she smiled. "But I don't care, as long as we get the sapphire back. Let's do it!"

Rachel took the squirt gun out of the bag while Kirsty checked to make sure that no one was coming.

"The coast is clear," she reported in a low voice.

Rachel handed the bag to Sophie. "Good luck!" she called as Sophie zoomed up into the air.

Then Rachel took the closed umbrella
in one hand. "Here goes!" she said, taking
a deep breath and
grabbing Kirsty's
arm with her
other hand.

Together, the
girls ran up the
steps toward
the pool. To their
relief, they saw
that the goblins
were still arguing.
They hadn't found
the sapphire yet!

"You nincompoop!"
one of them was shouting.

"Look who's talking, birdbrain!" the
other yelled back.

Holding the umbrella like a sword,
Rachel stepped into the water.

"*Arghhh!*" she screamed to startle the
goblins, who jumped and cried out in
alarm.

Kirsty stomped her feet, splashing water
around them. At the same moment,
Sophie dived down from the sky and
dropped the shopping bag neatly over
one goblin's head.

"Hey! What's going on?" he yelled, staggering around in the water. He couldn't see or get his hands free. "Everything is dark!"

Rachel swung the umbrella toward the other goblin. "Quick, Kirsty!" she cried. "Look for the jewel!"

The goblin saw Kirsty reach down to search for the sapphire at the bottom of the pool. He began to jump toward the

girls, splashing his big feet so that Kirsty couldn't see into the rippling water.

Rachel pressed the button on the umbrella's handle, and it suddenly snapped open to its full size, fending off the goblin's splashes.

"Whoa!" the goblin cried in surprise.

In the meantime, Kirsty was desperately feeling around the bottom of the pool, searching for the magic jewel. Her fingers closed on something smooth and round, and warm tingles shot up her arm. She caught her breath. She knew that feeling — it was fairy magic! "I've got

it!" she cried, pulling the sapphire from
the water and scrambling to her feet.

But just then, Sophie's voice echoed
through the air. "Watch out, girls!" she
cried from above.

A hard spray of water hit Kirsty in the
back. She gasped in surprise and turned
around.

A third goblin was standing on the
edge of the pool. In his hands was
Danny's turbo-charged squirt gun!

Goblin Attack!

"There's another goblin!" Kirsty gasped, remembering that she had seen three cherubs on the stone bowl of the fountain. The goblin holding the squirt gun must have jumped down from the fountain and snuck up behind her while she and Rachel were trying to keep his two goblin friends away.

"Give me that jewel!" the goblin yelled.
He was bigger than the other two and
even scarier, with a long nose and thick
eyebrows. He quickly refilled the squirt
gun in the pool and blasted the girls with
another burst of water.

Rachel staggered and dropped the
umbrella as the water hit her. "Hey!" she
cried, caught by surprise.

"I want that sapphire!" the goblin
shouted. "And if you don't hand it over,
I'll keep squirting you!"

Sophie darted down from the sky.
"Leave Rachel and Kirsty alone, you big
bully," she cried bravely. "The sapphire
is not yours. It belongs in Queen
Titania's crown!"

"Pesky little fairy!" the goblin growled.

He lifted his squirt gun and shot water at
Sophie, who squealed and dodged out of
the way just in time. The goblin fired
again. This time, Sophie just barely
missed getting hit by the water.

Rachel grabbed Kirsty's arm. "We
have to stop him!" she said anxiously. "If
the water hits Sophie, it will knock her
out of the sky!"

The goblin aimed the squirt gun at Sophie again.

"Stop it!" Rachel shouted, wading forward.

Kirsty followed her friend. "I have a plan, Rachel!" she hissed. "If we can reach the edge of the fountain, maybe we can knock him over. There's only one of him, and there are two of us!"

But just then, there was a triumphant yell from the middle of the pool. The girls spun around to see that the goblin under the shopping bag had wriggled free. His goblin friend grabbed the umbrella. Rachel had dropped it in all the confusion!

"You won't get away with the sapphire now!" the  goblin with the umbrella said as he splashed across the pool. The goblin with the squirt gun stepped into the water and began to wade toward the girls, too.

"We're trapped!" exclaimed Kirsty, realizing that all three goblins had surrounded them.

"Quick!" Sophie cried from high above. "There are people coming down the street. They'll see what's happening! We have to get out of here with the sapphire — now!"

Sapphire! The word echoed in Kirsty's mind. Of course! Why hadn't she thought of it before? She was holding a jewel full of wishing magic! She looked at the three goblins. Could she use the sapphire to stop them? Knowing that she had to try, Kirsty lifted the sparkling

stone and cried, "I wish . . ." She glanced
around for inspiration, and her gaze fell
on the mermaid's tail. "I wish you
goblins were all fish!"

Blue and silver sparks shot into the air.
As they streamed down over the goblins'
heads, there was a tinkling sound.
Suddenly, the three goblins vanished!

"Where did they go?" Rachel asked.
Then she looked down at the water and
gasped. "Oh!"

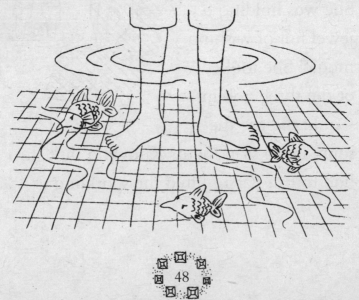

Kirsty stared into the pool. Three goldfish were swimming around her feet. They looked just like ordinary orange goldfish, except that they had extra-long pointed noses and very beady eyes! "The sapphire worked!" she said.

"Of course, it worked," Sophie cried, swooping down with a silvery laugh. "It's a wishing jewel, isn't it? What a great idea to use it like that, Kirsty!"

"Thanks," Kirsty said, smiling with relief. She bent down toward the water. "I hope you'll be very happy living here, little goblin-fish," she said cheerfully. The fish darted around her feet,

and Kirsty could have sworn that they
had grumpy frowns on their faces.

Giggling, the girls picked up the squirt
gun, umbrella, and shopping bag and
climbed out of the fountain.

"Just in time,"
Sophie said, settling
on Rachel's shoulder
and hiding under her
hair as a group of
shoppers walked by.

The girls sat down
on one of the
benches and tried to
look like they were just
chatting. Luckily, nobody
seemed to notice that they were
dripping wet!

As soon as the people had left the

square, Sophie peeked out from behind Rachel's hair. "Thanks for finding the sapphire," she said happily.

"I'm just glad we could help," said Rachel, shivering on the bench. She looked at the sparkling jewel in her hand. "It's beautiful!"

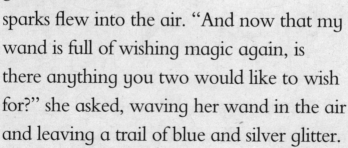

"I know," Sophie said, smiling. She touched her wand to the surface of the gem, and blue sparks flew into the air. "And now that my wand is full of wishing magic again, is there anything you two would like to wish for?" she asked, waving her wand in the air and leaving a trail of blue and silver glitter.

Kirsty and Rachel looked at each other. "We wish we were warm and dry again!" they cried at the same time.

"That's easy!" Sophie declared with an expert wave of her wand. Sparkles swirled around the girls and, within a second, their wish was granted.

"Thanks, Sophie," Rachel said gratefully, feeling much warmer.

"Will the goblins be OK as goldfish?" Kirsty asked.

"They'll be fine," Sophie assured her. "When Jack Frost learns that the sapphire has been returned to Fairyland, he'll come and find them. *That's* when they'll be in trouble."

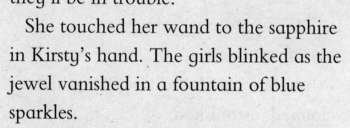

She touched her wand to the sapphire in Kirsty's hand. The girls blinked as the jewel vanished in a fountain of blue sparkles.

"It's safe in Fairyland now," Sophie said. "And I'd better follow it. Good-bye girls, and thank you for saving another one of our magic jewels." With that,

Sophie flapped her wings. But to Kirsty
and Rachel's surprise, she didn't fly into
the air! They saw a look of concern cross
Sophie's face. She flapped her wings
again. Nothing happened.

"My wings aren't working!" Sophie
exclaimed, astonished.

"What do you mean?" Kirsty asked.

"They won't lift me into the air,"
Sophie replied, looking panicky.

Kirsty looked down at the fairy's back.

Sophie's silvery wings seemed strangely faint. "Your wings look really pale, Sophie," she said.

"Yes, they're almost see-through," Rachel agreed. "It seems like they're . . . fading away."

"Fading away!" Sophie exclaimed. "But they can't be!" She stared at the girls in horror. "What's happening? Why can't I fly?"

Fairy Dust

"Maybe you're just tired," Rachel suggested hopefully. "You had to fly around a lot to avoid that squirt gun."

Sophie shook her head. "Fairies' wings don't fade when they get tired," she replied. Silver tears filled her eyes. "I think I must be sick."

"Or maybe . . ." Kirsty said, thinking

hard, ". . . it has something to do with the missing diamond."

"Oh, the diamond!" Rachel echoed. "It's the only magic jewel we haven't found yet."

Kirsty nodded. "Doesn't the diamond control flying magic, Sophie?"

"Yes," Sophie agreed.

"Well, maybe the fairies' flying magic is running low because the diamond is still missing," Kirsty suggested. "It might not be only your wings that are fading, Sophie. Maybe *all* the fairies' wings are fading!"

Sophie looked like she didn't know

whether to be relieved or even more
worried.

"I think you might be right, Kirsty!"
she gasped. "Our flying magic must be
running out!"

"We'll find the diamond," Kirsty told
her quickly. "Don't worry about that,
Sophie. But how are you going to get
home to Fairyland now?"

"I don't know," replied
Sophie, looking upset.
"How can I get back
without wings?"

"I have an idea,"
Rachel said. "We
could use some of
our fairy dust to send
you back!"

"Oh, yes!" Kirsty agreed. She pulled

out the golden locket she wore around
her neck. Rachel had a matching one.
"Queen Titania gave us these lockets,"
she told Sophie. "They're full of fairy
dust. We're supposed to use it if we ever
need to get to Fairyland."

"And is there any reason why the fairy
dust wouldn't work on a fairy?" Rachel
asked Sophie.

"No," said Sophie, grinning now. "In fact, I'm sure it would take me right back to Fairyland."

"Well, here goes . . ." Kirsty said, opening her locket and taking out a pinch of fairy dust.

"Thanks for all your help, girls," Sophie said. "I'll be sure to tell everyone how kind you've been."

Very gently, Kirsty sprinkled the dust over Sophie's head.

"Good-bye, Sophie!" she and Rachel said together.

The dust swirled around the tiny fairy, and Sophie smiled. "It's working! I can feel it. I'm off to Fairyland!" she called. With a happy wave, she disappeared.

"Phew," Kirsty said in relief. "At least Sophie's safely back home."

"Yes," Rachel agreed happily. "And so is the sapphire." Standing up, she put the squirt gun back into the shopping bag and picked up the umbrella. "It's been an exciting day."

"Almost *too* exciting," said Kirsty, looking at the fountain. "But now there's only one jewel left for us to find."

"We have to find it as soon as possible," Rachel pointed out. "The fairies need their flying magic back."

Kirsty nodded in agreement. It was awful to think of all their fairy friends,

unable to fly. "We'll find the diamond!"
she declared firmly. "Even Jack Frost
won't be able to stop us."

Rachel grinned. "Watch out, goblins.
Here we come!"

THE JEWEL FAIRIES

India, Scarlett, Emily, Chloe, Amy,
and Sophie all have their jewels back.
Now Rachel and Kirsty must help

Lucy the
Diamond Fairy!

Can they find the final jewel, and bring
the flying magic back to Fairyland?

Off to Fairyland!

Kirsty Tate folded her sweatshirt and put it into her bag. "There," she said to her best friend, Rachel Walker. "I'm all packed." She looked at the clock on Rachel's bedroom wall. "Six o'clock already!" Kirsty groaned. "Mom and Dad will be here to pick me up soon. I can't believe this week is almost over, can you?"

Rachel shook her head. "No," she replied. "It's gone so fast! But it's been a lot of fun."

The girls grinned at each other. Whenever they were together, the two of them always had the most wonderful adventures: fairy adventures! This week, the girls had been helping the Jewel Fairies find the seven magic jewels missing from Fairy Queen Titania's crown. So far, Kirsty and Rachel had found six of the stolen jewels — but the diamond was still missing.

Kirsty frowned. "I can't help feeling like something's wrong today," she said. "I was sure we'd find the magic diamond before I had to go home."

"Me, too," Rachel agreed. "And we haven't seen a fairy today, either. I

wonder if they're all trapped in Fairyland."

The girls exchanged worried glances. They both knew that the diamond controlled flying magic. Since it was missing, the fairies were starting to lose their ability to fly.

"We'll just have to go to Fairyland ourselves and find out!" Kirsty said in a determined voice.

Rachel nodded, and Kirsty quickly opened the locket that she always wore around her neck. Queen Titania had given the girls matching lockets full of fairy dust that would take them straight to Fairyland if ever they needed help. "Let's use our last pinches of fairy dust to get there," she suggested.

"Good idea," Rachel agreed. "Let's go!"

Both girls sprinkled the glittering golden dust over themselves. *Whoosh!* There was a fizzing sound, then everything blurred into a whirlwind of sparkling rainbow colors. The girls felt like they were tumbling through the air, shrinking smaller and smaller as they spun.

Moments later, they found themselves landing gently at the foot of a tall, twisting tree that stretched high above their heads. There in front of them stood King Oberon and Queen Titania, with all the Jewel Fairies.

"We're back in Fairyland," Kirsty cheered, "and we're fairy-size!" She flapped her shimmering wings happily. Being a fairy was fun!

"Welcome back, girls," King Oberon said warmly.

"Hello," Rachel replied, smiling. But Rachel's smile faded as she suddenly realized that something was terribly wrong. "Your Majesties!" she gasped, looking around. "Where are all the fairies' wings?"

There's Magic in Every Series!

The Rainbow Fairies

The Weather Fairies

The Jewel Fairies

The Pet Fairies

The Fun Day Fairies

The Petal Fairies

The Dance Fairies

Read them all!

■SCHOLASTIC

www.scholastic.com

www.rainbowmagiconline.com

HIT entertainment

RMFAIRY

SPECIAL EDITION

More Rainbow Magic Fun!
Three Stories in One!